小鼠拍檔康柏與小波的遊樂園之旅

cornbread & poppy at the carnival

馬修・科戴爾 Matthew Cordell／文圖

劉清彥／譯

三民書局

獻給蘿米和狄恩

小書芽

小鼠拍檔：康柏與小波的遊樂園之旅

文　　圖｜馬修．科戴爾
譯　　者｜劉清彥
責任編輯｜江奕萱

發 行 人｜劉仲傑
出 版 者｜弘雅三民圖書股份有限公司
地　　址｜臺北市復興北路 386 號（復北門市）
　　　　　臺北市重慶南路一段 61 號（重南門市）
電　　話｜(02)25006600
網　　址｜三民網路書店 https://www.sanmin.com.tw

出版日期｜初版一刷 2023 年 5 月
書籍編號｜H860380
I S B N｜978-626-307-978-6

弘雅三民圖書

目錄

天大的好消息

康柏好餓。這頓午餐，他最好的朋友小波已經遲到十一分鐘了。

「康柏，我有個天大的好消息！」小波終於出現在他家門口。康柏很愛小波，但每次小波有「天大的好消息」時，卻也總是讓他很擔心。

「請進，小波，」康柏說。「妳上次有天大的好消息時，我們看了那部妳想看的恐怖電影，害我連續作了一整個星期惡夢。」

康柏超級怕怪物。

「妳再前一次有天大的好消息時，我們去吃了妳想吃的可怕爆漿起司，害我反胃了好幾個小時。」

康柏超級怕爆漿起司。

「妳又再前一次有天大的好消息時，我們去了古老的鳌蝦洞穴探險……

結果我昏倒了。」

康柏超級怕黑。

「嗯，好嘛！但我的好消息不是每次都讓你生病或害怕呀，康柏！」小波說。那倒是真的。小波的好消息也不見得都帶來可怕的結果。

像是去溫克奶奶的農場摘覆盆子當零食。

或ㄏㄨㄛˋ是ㄕˋ坐ㄗㄨㄛˋ橡ㄒㄧㄤˋ皮ㄆㄧˊ鴨ㄧㄚ遊ㄧㄡˊ惠ㄏㄨㄟˋ普ㄆㄨˇ爾ㄦˇ溪ㄒㄧ 。

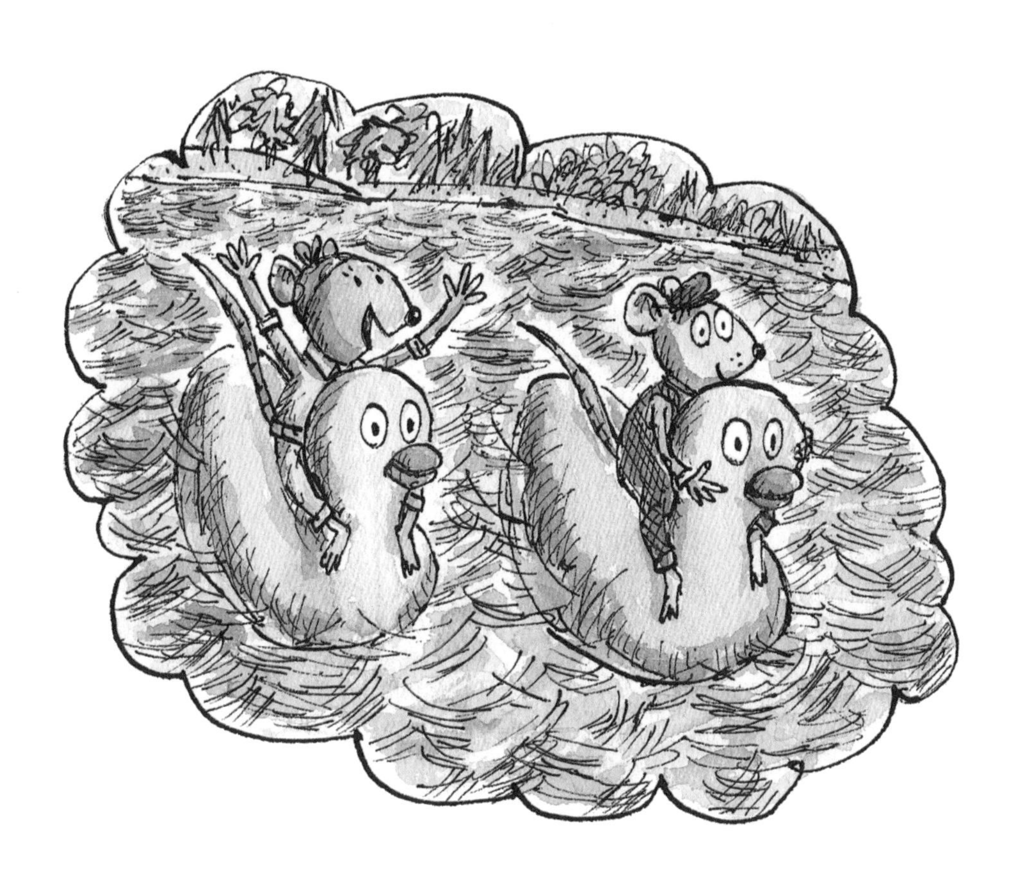

到鎮上的派對，隨著土撥鼠樂團的音樂跳舞。

「好吧，」康柏同意了。

「什麼好消息？」

「遊樂園來鎮上了！」小波大聲叫喊。

「遊樂園是什麼？」康柏問。

小波很驚訝。「你從來沒有去過遊樂園？」

「遊樂園有賣糖果和點心……」

「嗯……糖果和點心，」康柏說。

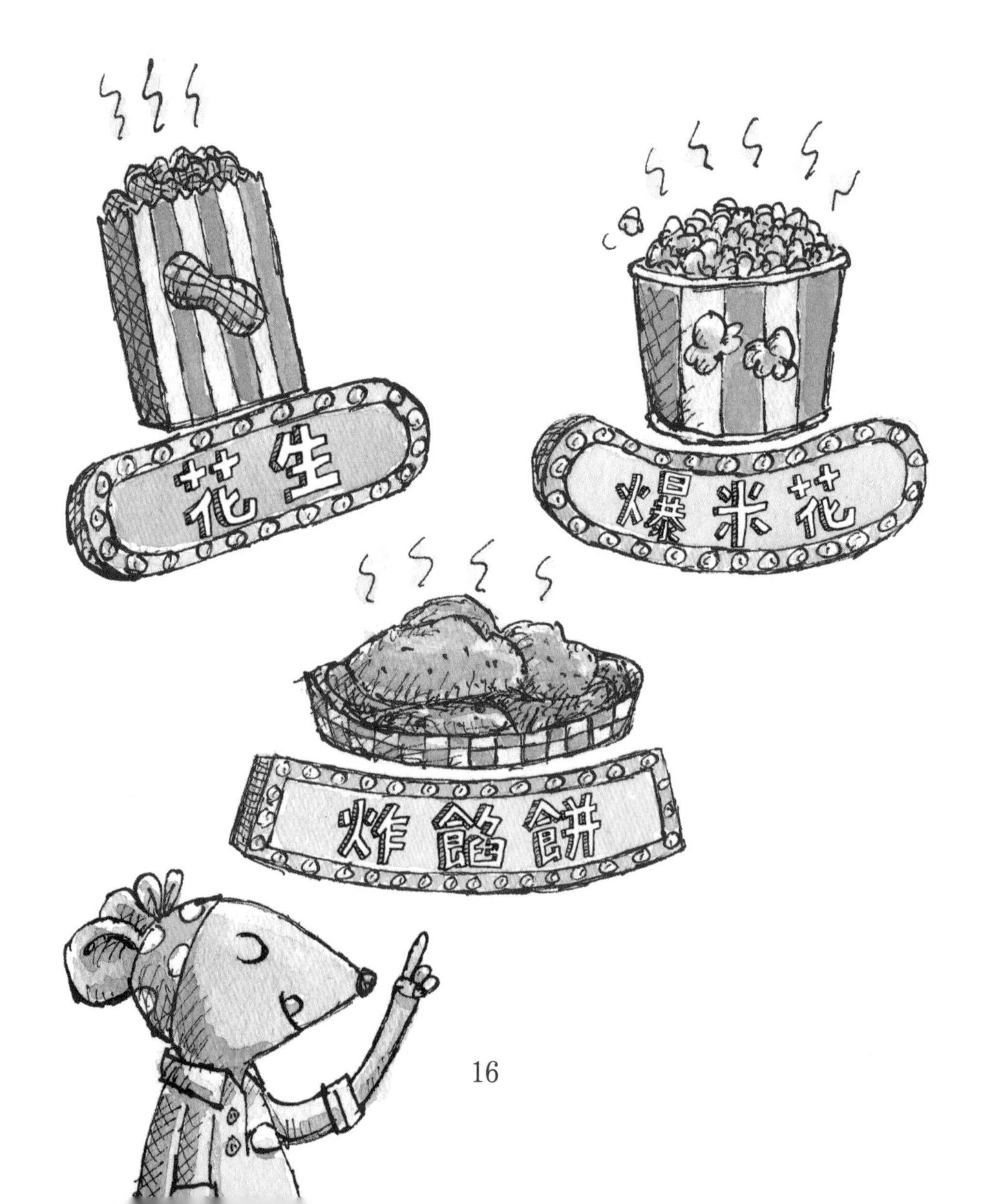

「還有遊戲和獎品……」

「我很喜歡遊戲。」康柏說。

「甚至還有高空飛行和急速飛車！」

「哎呀。」康柏說。

「哎呀什麼？」

小波說。

「我不要急速也不要高空！聽起來好大、好快，只要轉錯一個彎，我們就…… ㄆㄧㄚ被壓扁了。」

「喔，康柏，」小波說。「不會被壓扁啦。那些遊樂設施都有專業的操作員在控制。總之，我會保護你！」

「真的嗎？」康柏問。

「當然啊！記得你看完電影被嚇壞的時候嗎？我在你的床邊睡了一整個星期耶。」

「嗯，是啦……」

「還有，那個超級美味的爆漿起司讓你反胃時，我幫你煮了薑茶，還為你唱了溫柔的搖籃曲，直到你感覺舒服一些。」

「嗯，是啦……」

「還有還有，你在古老的螯蝦洞穴裡昏倒時，我可是一路背著你走出來喔。」

「對，小波，那個我記得，」康柏說。「謝謝妳保護我。」

「也謝謝你願意和我嘗試新的事物！」小波說。「所以要去遊樂園嗎？」

「去遊樂園吧！」康柏同意。

「這真是個天大的好消息！」

「可是，先……吃午餐吧！」康柏說。

遊樂園

「哇，鎮上的所有居民一定都來了！」小波叫喊。

在瑪姬山谷裡有帳篷、攤位和大型遊樂設施。各種動物蜂擁而入，四處逛著遊樂園。

「康柏，我們趕快下去看看遊樂園吧！」

他們在入口處付了兩塊錢給賣門票的獾。

他們在裡面見到了許多熟悉和不熟悉的面孔。

大象一家正吃著一大袋的烤花生。

賽伯和豪斯費勒正在排隊等棉花糖。

康柏和小波驚訝的發現，就連鎮上脾氣最壞的老賴瑞，都把自己拖下床來遊樂園了。

「絕對不能錯過！」老賴瑞邊說邊津津有味的嚼著炸蘋果餡餅。

「康柏，我們去吃炸餡餅吧！」小波說。

康柏從來沒有聽過炸餡餅這種東西，可是它的味道好香，看起來也好好吃。

「太ㄊㄞˋ好ㄏㄠˇ吃ㄔ了ㄌㄜ！」康ㄎㄤ柏ㄅㄛˊ說ㄕㄨㄛ。甜ㄊㄧㄢˊ甜ㄊㄧㄢˊ熱ㄖㄜˋ熱ㄖㄜˋ，外ㄨㄞˋ酥ㄙㄨ內ㄋㄟˋ軟ㄖㄨㄢˇ，還ㄏㄞˊ有ㄧㄡˇ奶ㄋㄞˇ油ㄧㄡˊ的ㄉㄜ滑ㄏㄨㄚˊ潤ㄖㄨㄣˋ和ㄏㄢˋ香ㄒㄧㄤ氣ㄑㄧˋ。

「快來啊！」附近攤位的豬大聲嚷嚷著。「通通有獎！」

小波付錢給豬，她拿到三個圈環，準備套瓶子。

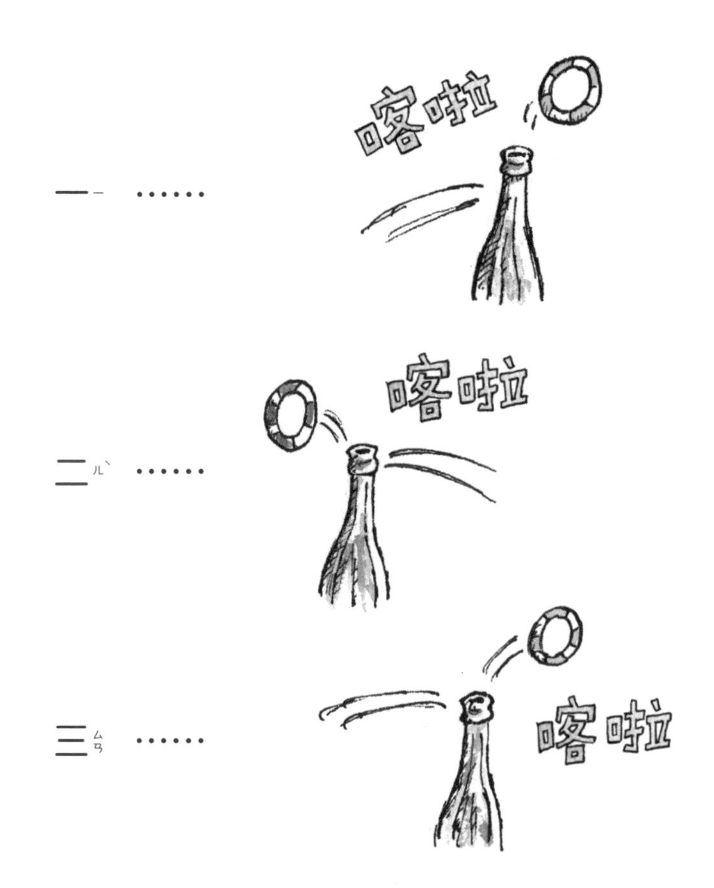

「通通有獎！」豬高聲叫嚷，他給了小波一個歪掉的瓶蓋。

「這算什麼獎品嘛。」小波不像剛剛那麼開心了。

「我試試看，」康柏說。
「我很愛玩遊戲。」

他付錢給豬。

一……

二……

三……

「通通有獎！」豬高聲叫嚷，他給了康柏一根巨大的絨毛香蕉。

「小_{ㄒㄧㄠ}波_{ㄅㄛ}，送_{ㄙㄨㄥ}妳_{ㄋㄧ}。」康_{ㄎㄤ}柏_{ㄅㄛ}笑_{ㄒㄧㄠ}嘻_{ㄒㄧ}嘻_{ㄒㄧ}的_{ㄉㄜ}把_{ㄅㄚ}獎_{ㄐㄧㄤ}品_{ㄆㄧㄣ}送_{ㄙㄨㄥ}給_{ㄍㄟ}小_{ㄒㄧㄠ}波_{ㄅㄛ}。

呼咻

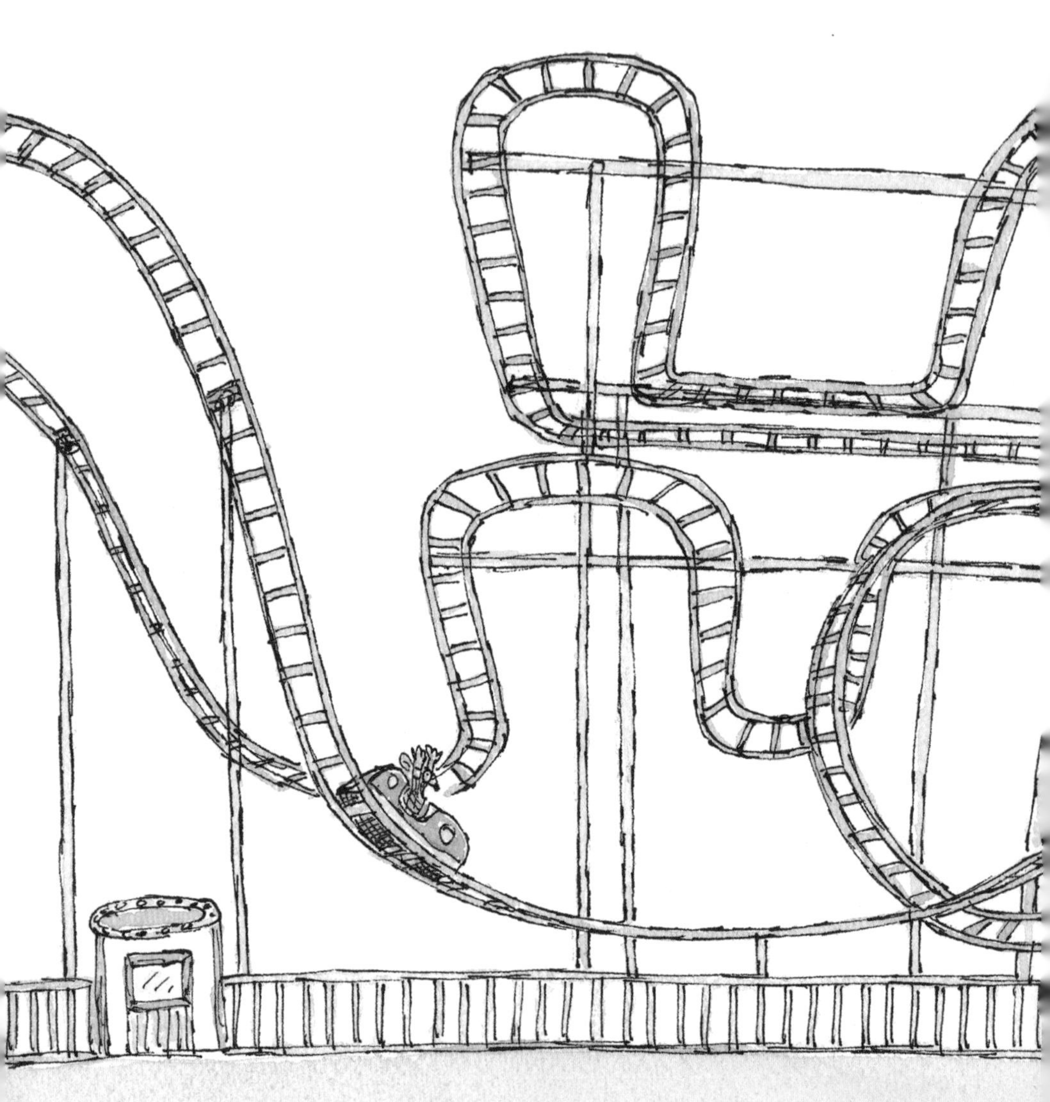

雲霄飛車從一旁的軌道飛馳而過。「哎呀。」康柏說。

「我們去坐碎骨飛車吧！」

小波說。

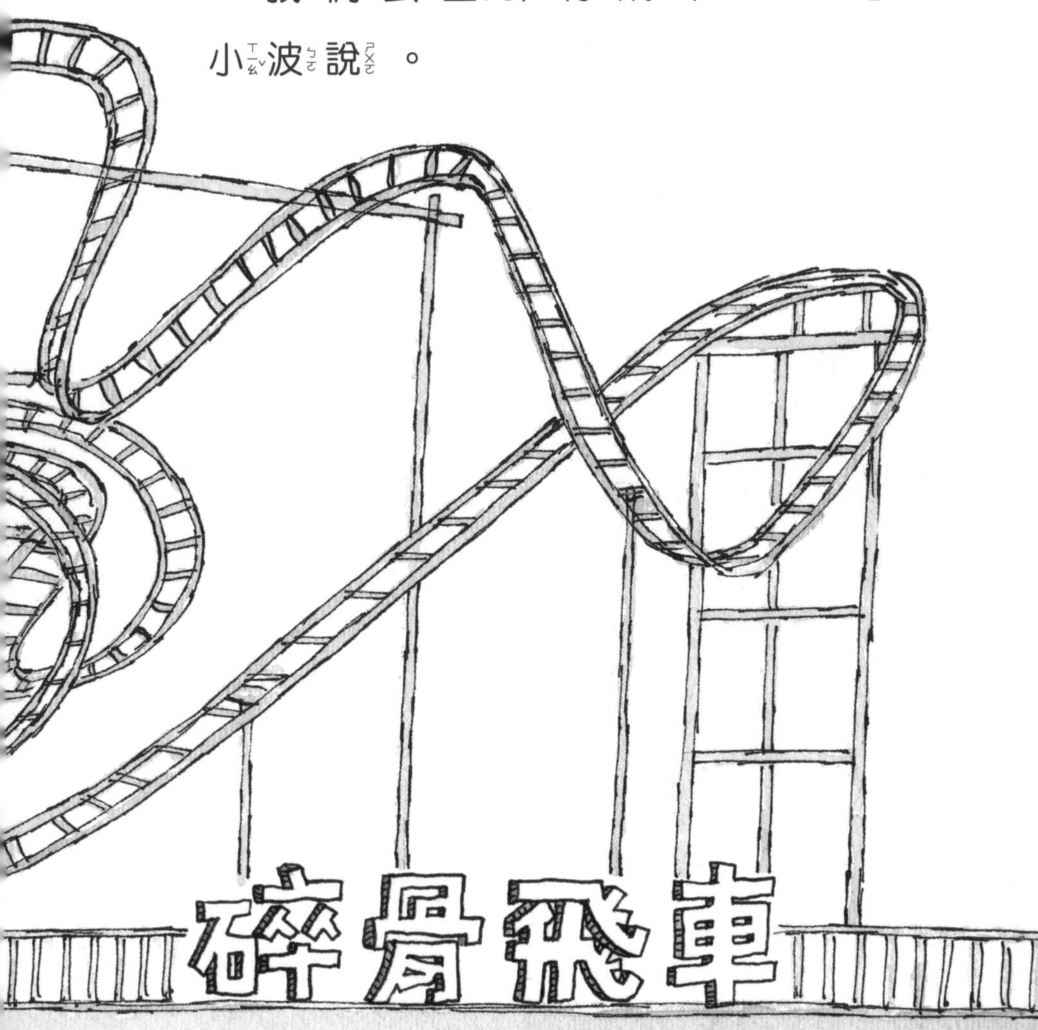

「想都別想。」

康柏說。

「想坐嘔吐飛輪嗎？」小波問。

「一點都不想。」康柏說。

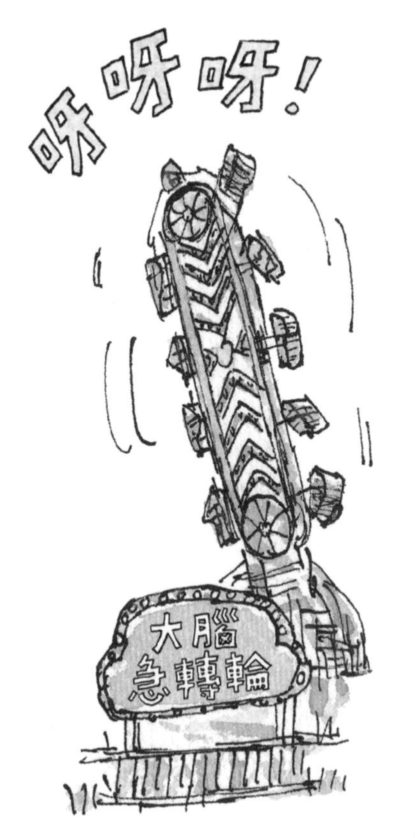

「那大腦急轉輪呢？」

「不要。」

「康柏，拜託和我坐一次嘛，摩天輪怎麼樣？」

「嗯……摩天輪聽起來還不錯，也比較平靜。小波，我可以和妳坐那個。」

他們走向遊樂園的另一邊。

「好大啊！」康柏大叫。

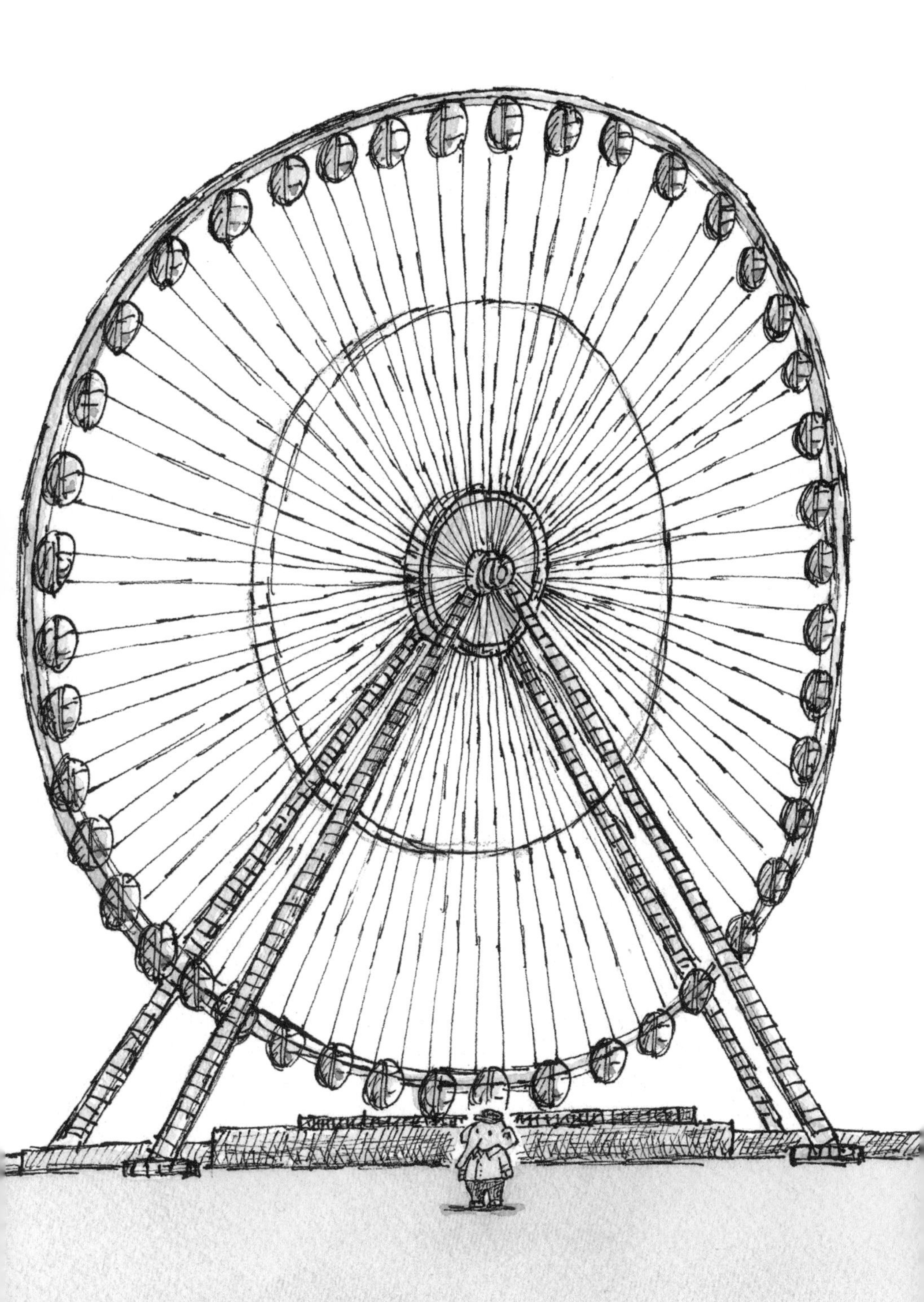

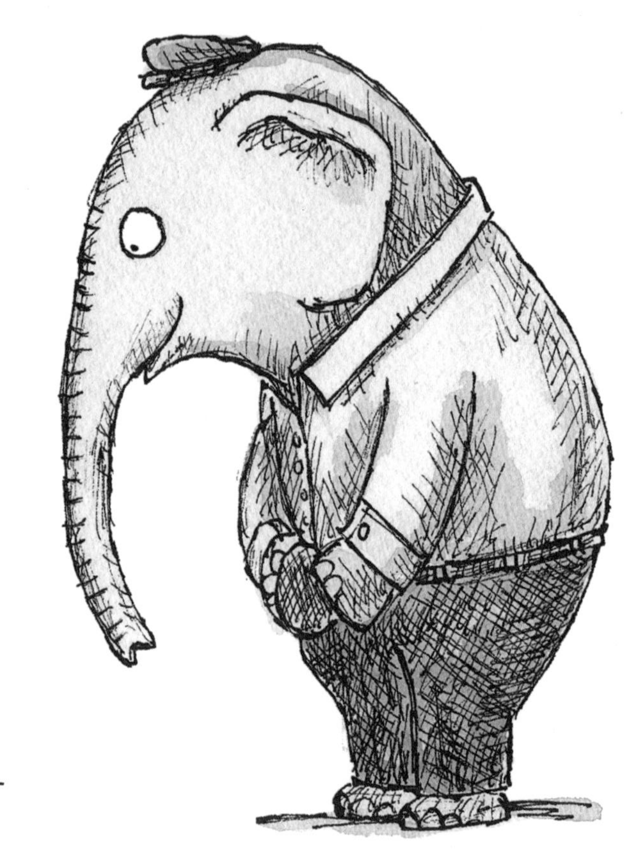

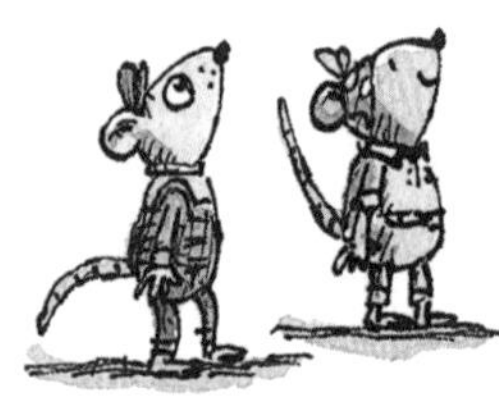

「這是ㄕˋ大ㄉㄚˋ象ㄒㄧㄤˋ尺ㄔˇ寸ㄘㄨㄣˋ的ㄉㄜ˙ ！」
大ㄉㄚˋ象ㄒㄧㄤˋ操ㄘㄠ作ㄗㄨㄛˋ員ㄩㄢˊ說ㄕㄨㄛ。

康柏和小波爬進巨大的車廂，繫緊安全帶。

摩天輪開始轉動，

他們越升越高……

也離地面

越來越遠。

不過，出乎意料之外……康柏竟然不害怕。

摩天輪緩慢平穩的轉動，他從來沒有在這麼高的地方看整個小鎮。真是太驚人了！

「小波，妳看！可以看見溫克奶奶的農場耶！」

他看向小波。小波緊閉著眼睛。

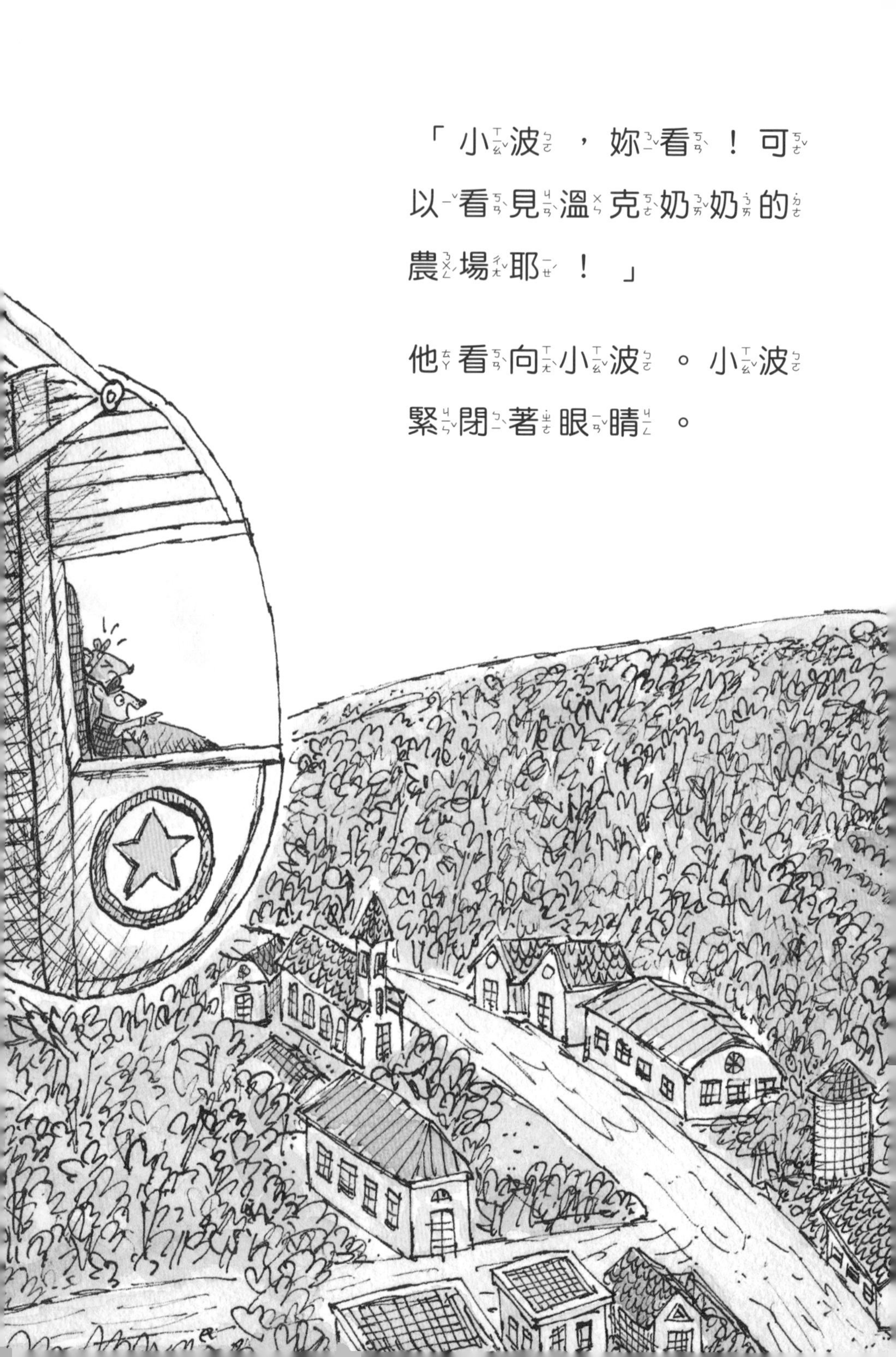

「小波，妳看！惠普爾溪耶！」

小波的眼睛甚至閉得更緊了。

「小波！是古老的螯蝦洞穴耶！」

「康柏！」小波大叫。

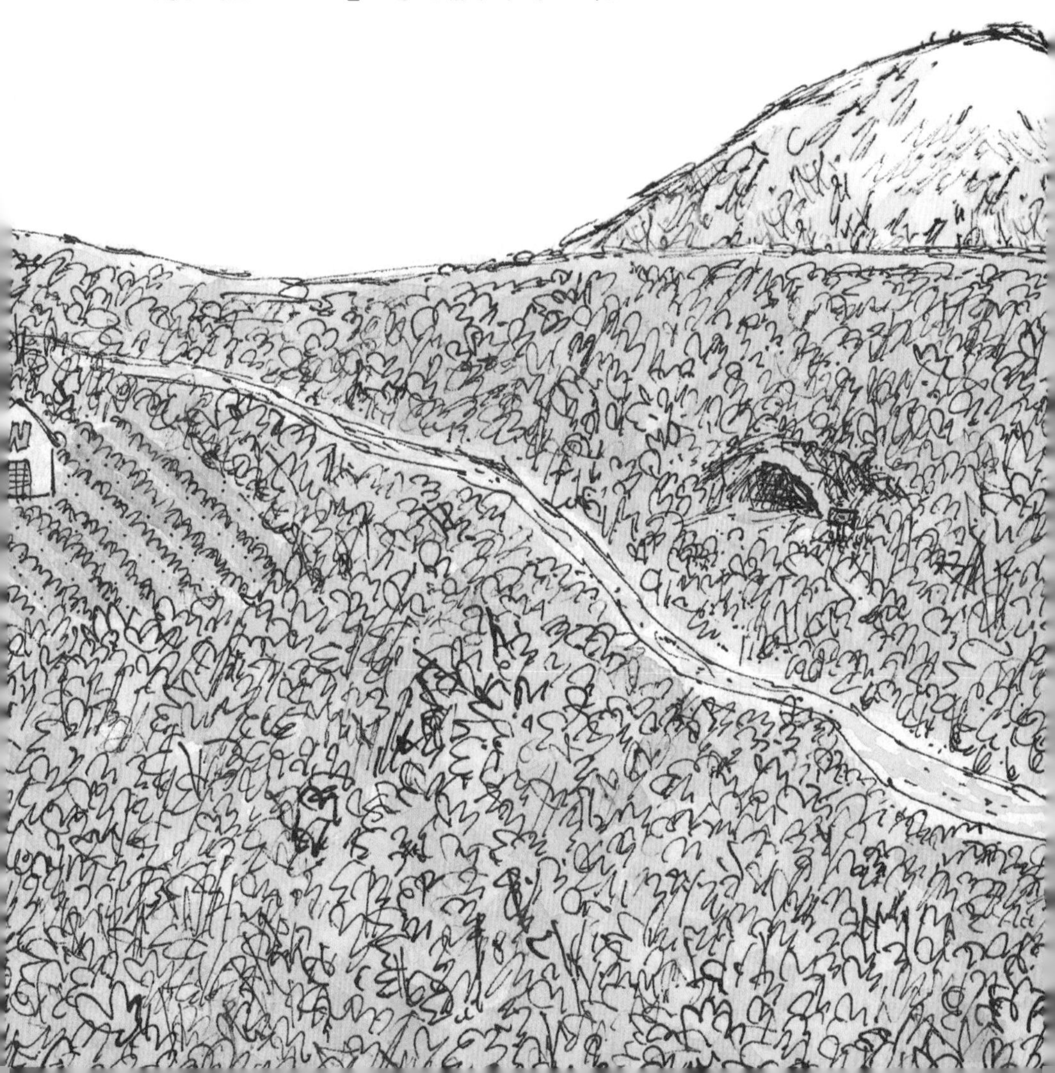

摩天輪

……我超怕高！

高！

高！

康柏緊緊握住小波的手。

「我保護妳，小波。」他說。

他們又繞了幾圈，直到摩天輪停下來。

「康柏，謝謝你。」小波說。

「不客氣，小波。」康柏說。

「我喜歡遊樂園！也很喜歡坐摩天輪！」

「太棒了！那我們去玩腸胃打結球！」小波叫嚷。

「想都別想。」康柏說。

花生

他們要離開遊樂園時，康柏注意到一個東西。

「小波，妳看，妳的腳踏車旁邊有一個花生。」

「康柏，你買了花生給我嗎？」小波問。「謝謝你！我超級愛吃花生！」

「我也愛花生，小波。可是我沒有買，」康柏說。「它就……在那裡。」

「喔ㄛ，太ㄊㄞˋ棒ㄅㄤˋ了˙ㄌㄜ！我ㄨㄛˇ等ㄉㄥˇ不ㄅㄨˋ及ㄐㄧˊ要ㄧㄠˋ吃ㄔ掉ㄉㄧㄠˋ它ㄊㄚ，我ㄨㄛˇ快ㄎㄨㄞˋ餓ㄜˋ扁ㄅㄧㄢˇ了˙ㄌㄜ。」小ㄒㄧㄠˇ波ㄅㄛ說ㄕㄨㄛ。

康ㄎㄤ柏ㄅㄛˊ也ㄧㄝˇ好ㄏㄠˇ餓ㄜˋ。

「其實……」康柏決定了，「我認為那個花生是我的，畢竟是我先發現它的。」

「沒錯，康柏，但是它在**我的**腳踏車旁邊。不管是誰留下來的，他應該就是要給**我**。」

小波伸手去拿花生。

「對啦，可是說不定……」康柏邊說邊阻止他的朋友，「花生的主人只是暫時把它放在這裡，這樣他們才能休息一下。這顆花生很大，我們應該等一等，說不定它的主人會回來拿。」

他們開始等。

過了十秒鐘。

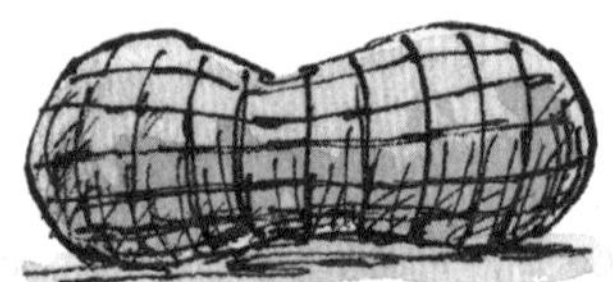

「好吧，它的主人沒有回來。因為是我先發現的，所以這顆花生是我的。」

「才怪，康柏，這是**我**的花生！」

接著，情況越來越糟。

小波大吼大叫說她有多麼喜歡花生，而且知道該怎麼享用這顆花生，所以是她——而不是他——有資格得到這顆花生。

接著，康柏也大吼大叫說他有多麼喜歡花生，自己還是小鼠寶寶的時候，就吃了第一顆花生，而且小時候，還是他告訴小波花生有多麼美味。所以是**他**——而不是**她**——有資格得到這顆花生。

他們繞著花生走來走去，直到……

好啦！
跺腳

小波氣呼呼的走開。

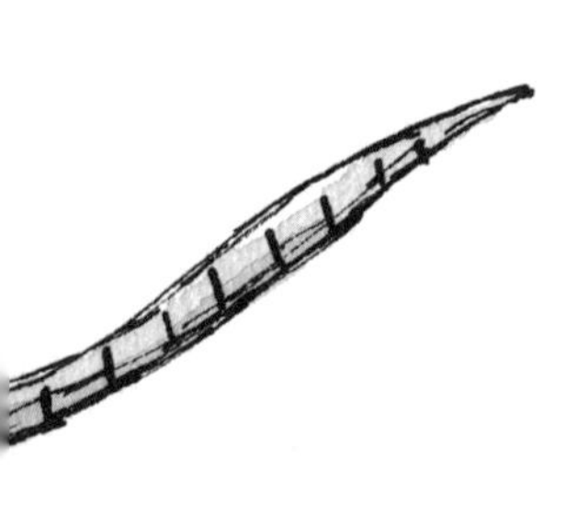

康柏氣呼呼的走開。

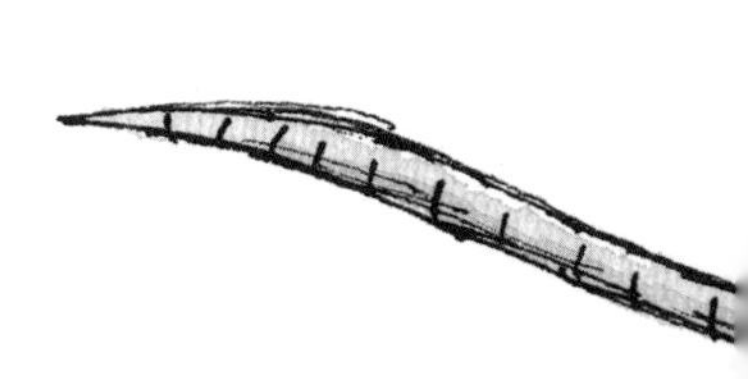

十秒鐘後，

小波好孤單。

康柏好孤單。

他們同時回頭看著那顆花生。

花生殼裡面有兩顆花生仁……

花生殼外面有兩個好朋友……

「嗨，康柏。」

「嗨，小波。」

「我們可以一起剝開它嗎？」他們異口同聲說。

哎呀

康柏擁抱小波，
小波也擁抱康柏。

「分享讓花生更美味！」
小波說。

砰！
砰！
砰！

一根巨大的象鼻把花生吸走了。

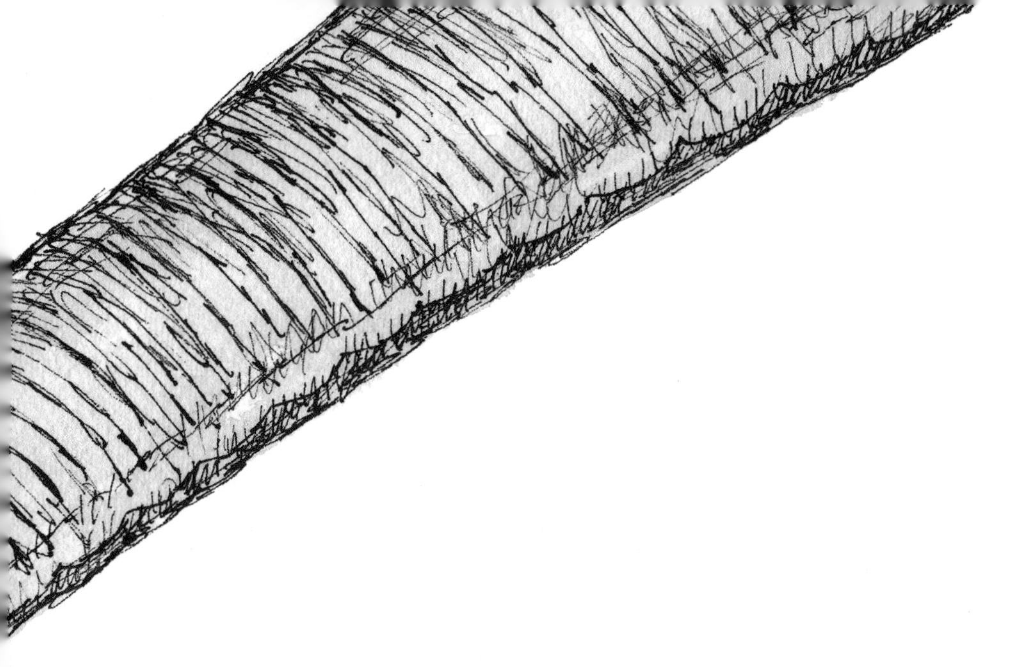

「謝謝囉！」摩天輪操作員說。

「明年遊樂園見！」

小波嘆了口氣。

康柏也嘆了口氣。

「小波，妳想吃起司嗎？那裡有賣妳喜歡的那種起司。」

「好啊，走吧。」

小波點了爆漿起司。

康柏點了巧達起司。

cornbread & poppy

at the carnival

matthew cordell

To Romy and Dean

Contents

The Best News Ever

Cornbread was hungry. His best friend, Poppy, was eleven minutes late for lunch.

"Cornbread, I have the best news!" said Poppy, finally arriving at his door. Cornbread loved Poppy, but he always worried when she had "the best news."

"Come in, Poppy," Cornbread said. "The last time you had the best news, we saw that terrible movie you wanted to see. I had nightmares for a week."

Cornbread was afraid of monsters.

“The time before that when you had the best news, we ate that terrible runny cheese you wanted to eat. It upset my stomach for hours.”

Cornbread was afraid of runny cheese.

"And the time before that when you had the best news, we explored the old Crawdad Caverns...

…and I fainted."

Cornbread was afraid of the dark.

“Okay, fine! But not all my news makes you sick and scared, Cornbread!” said Poppy.

It was true. Poppy often had news of things that didn’t end terribly.

Like snacking on raspberries at Grandma Winkle’s farm.

Like sailing down Whipple Creek
on rubber ducks.

Like dancing to the Marmot Band at the big town Barn Buster.

"Okay," Cornbread allowed.

"What is it?"

“The Carnival is in town!” shouted Poppy.

“What’s the Carnival?” asked Cornbread.

Poppy was surprised. “You’ve never been to the Carnival?!”

"At the Carnival, there's sweets and treats...."

"Mmm...sweets and treats," said Cornbread.

"Games and prizes..."

"I do like games," said Cornbread.

"There's even high-flying, zooming rides!"

"Uh-oh," said Cornbread.

"Uh-oh?" said Poppy.

"I am not going to zoom, and I am not going to fly! That sounds terribly big and terribly fast, and just one wrong turn and we're… SQUOOSH."

"Oh, Cornbread," said Poppy. "There is no SQUOOSH. These rides are operated by professionals. And anyway, I'll protect you!"

"You will?" asked Cornbread.

"Of course! Remember when you were scared after that movie? I slept by your bed for a week."

"Well, yes..."

“And when that fabulous runny cheese didn’t agree with you? I made you ginger tea and sang you sweet lullabies till you were better.”

“Well, yes…”

"And remember when you fainted in the old Crawdad Caverns? I carried you all the way out on my back."

"Hmm. Yes, I do remember that, Poppy," said Cornbread. "Thank you for protecting me."

"And thank you for doing new things with me!" said Poppy. "So... to the Carnival?"

"To the Carnival!" Cornbread agreed.

"That's the best news ever!"

"But first...lunch!" said Cornbread.

The Carnival

"Wow, the whole town must be here!" Poppy exclaimed.

Down at the base of Maggie Valley, there were tents and booths and great big mechanical moving structures. Animals of all kinds swarmed in and around it all.

"Let's get down there and see the Carnival, Cornbread!"

At the entrance, they paid two hay pennies to a badger to get in.

Inside, they saw both familiar and not-so-familiar faces.

An elephant family was snacking on a gigantic bag of roasted peanuts.

Sable and Horsefeather were waiting in line for cotton candy.

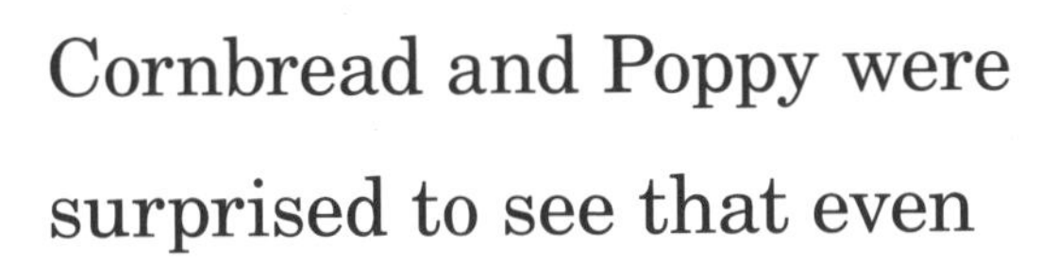

Cornbread and Poppy were surprised to see that even Old Larry, the town grump, had pulled himself out of bed to visit the Carnival.

“Wouldn’t miss it!” said Old Larry, munching a fried apple fritter.

"Let's get a fritter, Cornbread!" said Poppy.

Cornbread had never even heard of a fritter.

But it smelled and looked delicious.

“Yum!” Cornbread said. It was warm and buttery, sweet and crispy on the outside and soft on the inside.

"Step right up!" barked a pig from a nearby booth. "Every player is a winner!"

Poppy paid the pig, and she was given three rings to toss and try to land on a bottle.

One...

Two...

Three...

“Every player is a winner!” barked the pig, and he gave Poppy a dented bottle cap.

“Not much of a winner,” said Poppy, a little less happy than before.

"Let me try," said Cornbread.

"I do love games."

He paid the pig.

One…

Two…

Three…

Clink!

"Every player is a winner!" barked the pig, and he gave Cornbread a giant plush banana.

"For you, Poppy." Cornbread smiled, giving Poppy his prize.

WHOOSH

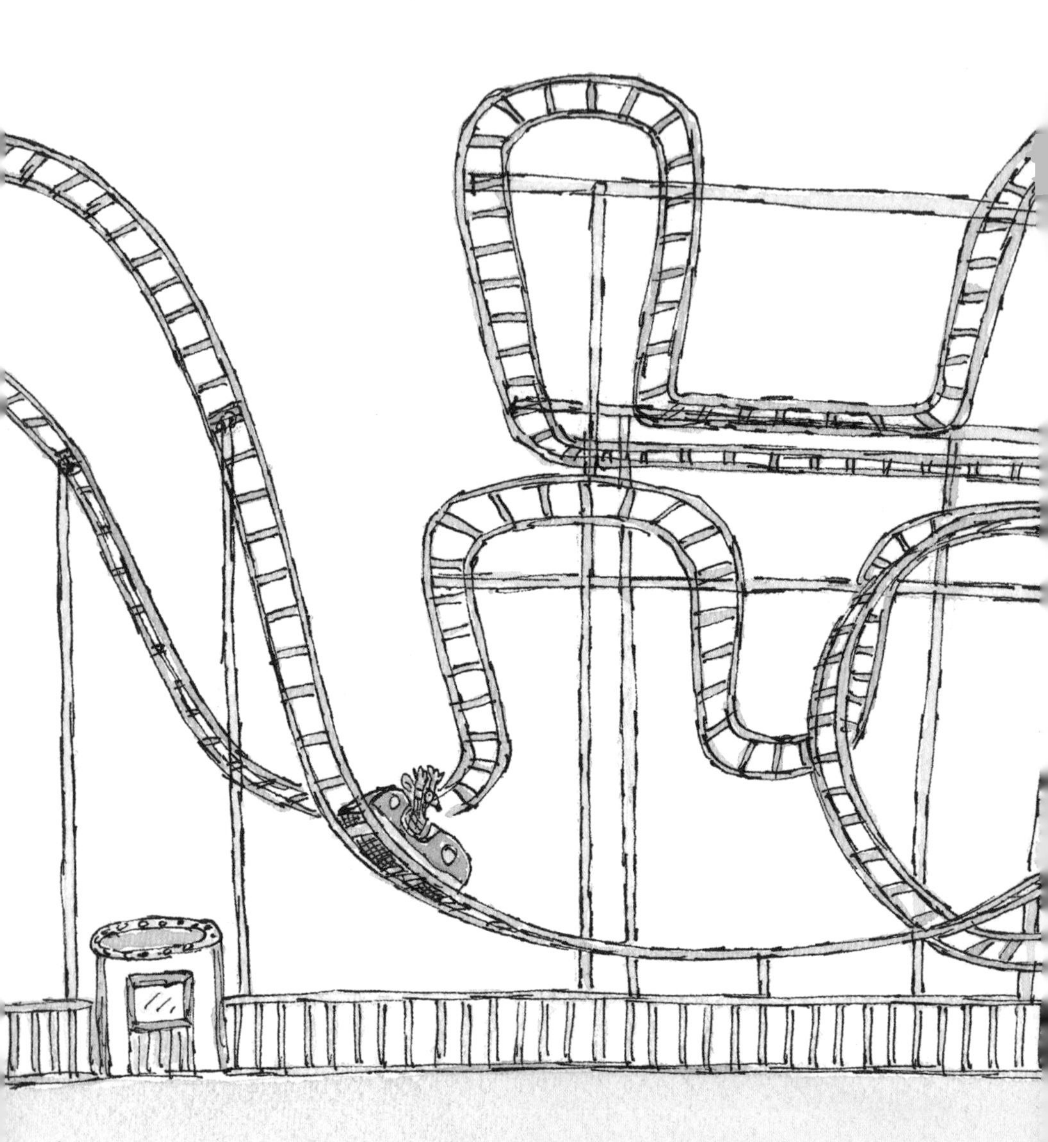

A roller coaster zoomed by on some nearby tracks. “Uh-oh,” said Cornbread.

“Let’s go on the Boneshaker!” Poppy exclaimed.

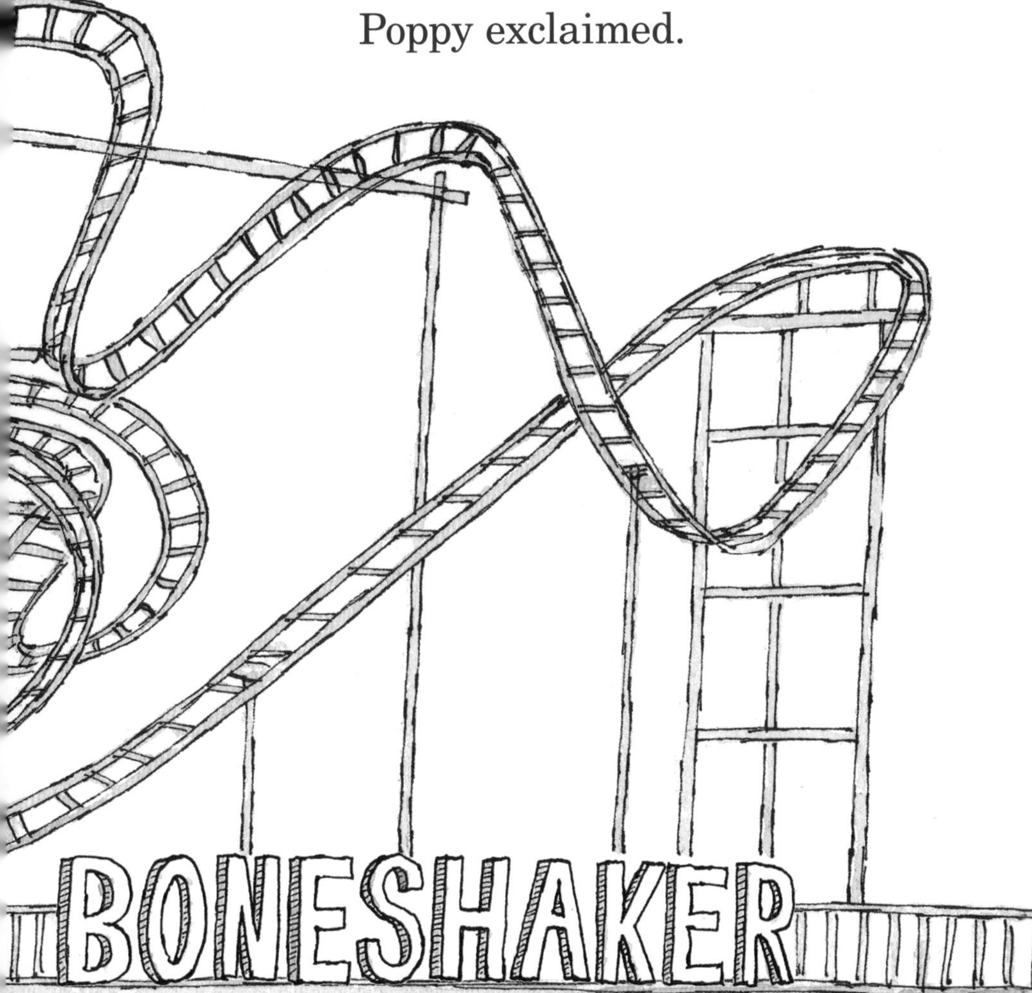

“No way,” said Cornbread.

"Want to ride
the Nauseator?"
asked Poppy.

"Not a chance,"
said Cornbread.

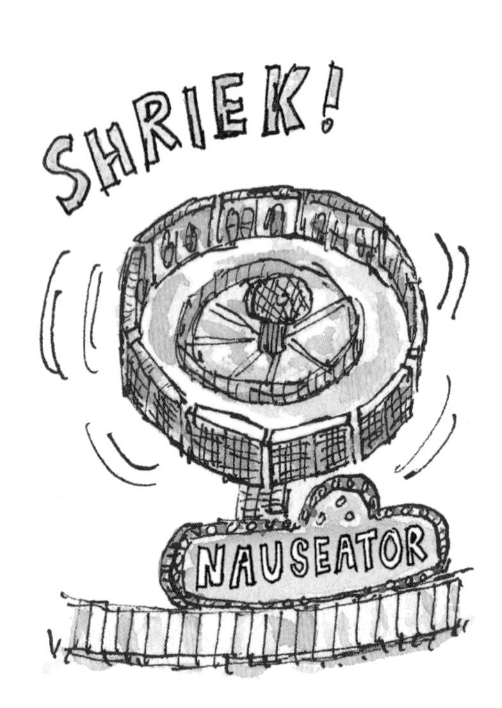

"How about the
Brain Tweaker?"

"Nope."

"Will you please ride one ride with me, Cornbread? What about the Ferris wheel over there?"

"Well…a Ferris wheel sounds nice and calm. I will ride that with you, Poppy."

They walked to the other side of the Carnival.

"It's huge!" cried Cornbread.

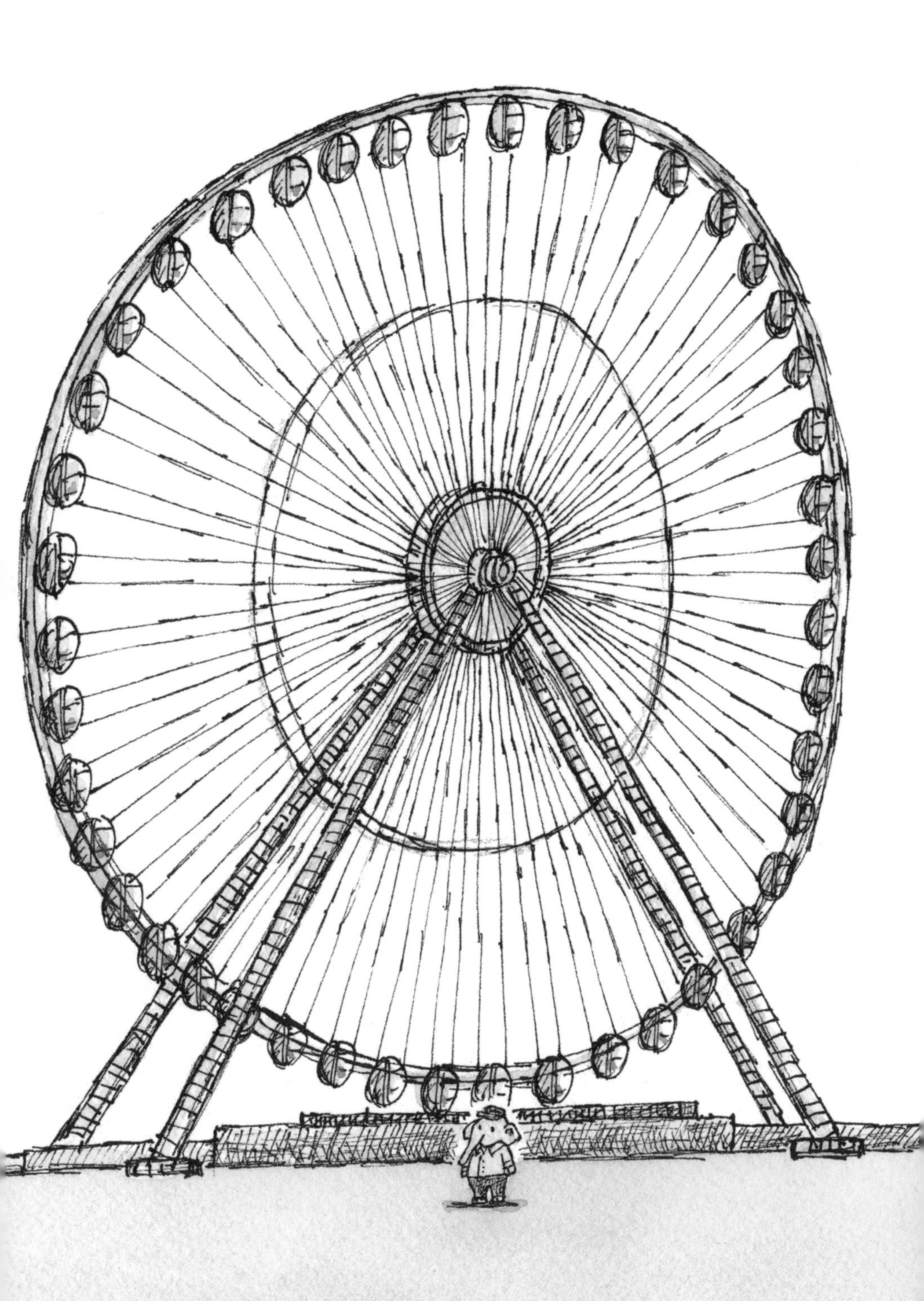

“Elephant-size!” said the elephant operator.

Cornbread and Poppy climbed into the giant gondola. They pulled their seat belts tight.

The wheel began to turn, and
they rose higher…

...and higher off the ground.

But surprisingly...

Cornbread wasn't afraid. The ride was smooth and slow, and he had never seen the town from this high up. It was amazing!

"Poppy, look! You can see Grandma Winkle's farm!"

He looked over at Poppy. Her eyes were closed.

“Poppy, look! Whipple Creek!”

Poppy screwed her eyes closed even tighter.

“Poppy! There’s the old Crawdad Caverns!”

“Cornbread!” Poppy yelled.

FERRIS
WHEEL

... I'm scared of **heights!**

heights!

heights!

Cornbread reached over. He squeezed Poppy's hand.

"I'll protect you, Poppy," he said.

They rode around a few more times until the wheel stopped.

"Thank you, Cornbread," said Poppy.

"You're welcome, Poppy," said Cornbread.
"I like the Carnival! I like rides!"

"Great! Let's go on the Gutbuster!" shouted Poppy.

“Not a chance,” said Cornbread.

The Peanut

As they were about to leave the Carnival, Cornbread noticed something.

"Poppy, look, there's a peanut by your bike."

"You bought me a peanut, Cornbread?" asked Poppy. "Thank you! I love peanuts!"

"I love peanuts too, Poppy. But I didn't buy it," Cornbread said. "It was just…there."

“Oh, goody! I can’t wait to eat it. I’m starved,” Poppy said.

Cornbread was starved too.

“Actually…,” Cornbread decided, “I think I should have the peanut. I’m the one who found it, after all.”

“Yes, Cornbread, but it was by MY bike. Whoever left it wanted ME to have it.”

Poppy reached for the peanut.

“Yes, but maybe…,” Cornbread said, stopping his friend, “someone just put it down here so they could rest for a minute. It is a big peanut. We should wait to see if someone comes back for it.”

They waited.

For ten seconds.

"Okay, they aren't coming back. So, since I found the peanut, I think I should have the peanut."

“No, Cornbread, it’s MY peanut!”

Then things got worse.

Poppy yelled and screamed about how much she loved peanuts and about all the ways she could prepare the peanut, and why SHE—not HE—deserved the peanut.

Then Cornbread yelled and screamed about how he loved peanuts and about how he was just a baby mouse when he first had a peanut and how he was the one to introduce Poppy to peanuts when they were just baby mice, and because of that HE—not SHE—deserved the peanut.

And they went back and forth and back and forth about the peanut until…

FINE!!
STOMP

Poppy stormed off.

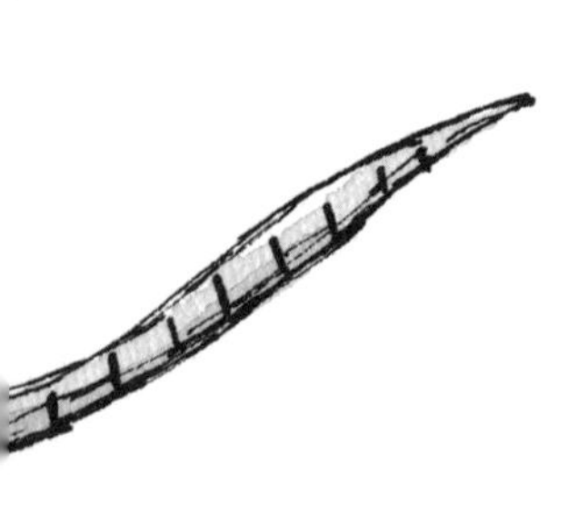

Cornbread stormed off.

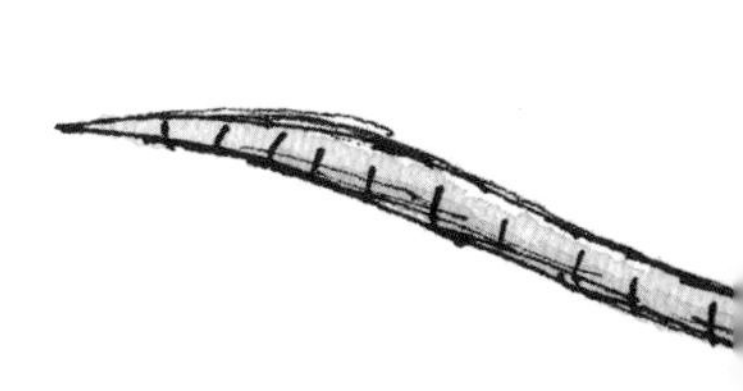

Ten seconds passed.

Poppy was alone.

Cornbread was alone.

They both looked back at the peanut.

Inside the shell, there were two nuts....

Outside the shell, there were two friends....

"Hi, Cornbread."

"Hi, Poppy."

"Can we split it?" they both said.

YIKES

Cornbread hugged Poppy, and Poppy hugged Cornbread.

“Sharing will make it taste better!” said Poppy.

BOOM!
BOOM!
BOOM!

A mighty elephant trunk sucked up the peanut.

“Thanks for the peanut!” said the Ferris wheel operator. “See you next year at the Carnival!”

Poppy sighed.

Cornbread sighed.

“Do you want to get some cheese, Poppy? They have the kind you like.”

“Yes, please.”

Poppy ordered the runny kind.

Cornbread got the cheddar.